D1302372

A sweet, sweet basket,
Clary, Margie Willis,

A Sweet, Sweet Basket

A Sweet, Sweet Basket

by Margie Willis Clary

illustrations by Dennis L. Brown

SANDLAPPER PUBLISHING CO., INC.

Second Printing 1996

Published by Sandlapper Publishing Co., Inc.
Orangeburg, South Carolina

Book design by Barbara Stone

Art consultant: Dorothy Ariail Welch

Printed in Canada

Library of Congress Cataloging-in-Publication Data

Clary, Margie Willis, 1931–
A sweet, sweet basket / by Margie Willis Clary.
p. cm.
Summary: Continuing a tradition that started in Africa, Grandma teaches Keisha how to weave a basket from South Carolina sweet grass.
ISBN 0-87844-127-1
[1. Basket making—Fiction. 2. Grandmothers—Fiction. 3. Afro-Americans—Fiction. 4. South Carolina—Fiction.] I. Title.
PZ7.C5627Sw 1995
[Fic]—dc20 94-39551
CIP
AC

This book is lovingly
dedicated to
my grandchildren
Caleb, Jill, and Scott.

Special thanks to

Minnie Brown
of Charleston, South Carolina
who served as the model for Grandma

and

the late Florence Mazyck's family of basket weavers
of Mount Pleasant, South Carolina
who provided weaving demonstrations and information

A Sweet, Sweet Basket

Keisha picked up her books as the school bus came to a stop. It had been a good day at school. However, with the warm spring weather, it was difficult to keep her mind on studying. It had been especially hard today as she was anxious to be home. Today was the day that Grandma reopened the basket stand on the highway.

Peering through the bus window, Keisha caught a glimpse of Grandma's straw hat and the tin roof of the basket stand laden with sweetgrass baskets. To the seven year old, there seemed to be a hundred baskets hanging on the stand. Grandma had worked many a long hour during the winter months getting ready for this day.

Keisha stepped from the bus. She looked both ways and walked carefully down the incline to the path that led to the white house in the pines. Her brother Raymond was behind her. They walked in silence until they reached the steps of the house.

"This is the day," Keisha said. "Wonder if Grandma's had any customers."

"Wonder if she made any money," Raymond remarked.

Throwing her books upon the steps, Keisha glanced toward her brother. "There's only one way to know. I'm going to the stand and find out. Come on with me."

"Can't go. Big Papa is out back plowing the garden and he promised to pay me five bucks to help him this afternoon. Anyway, basket weaving is woman's work." Raymond turned and headed to the back of the house.

Schoo

Keisha walked up the path beside the busy highway. She jumped over a limb of yellow jasmine that grew along the path. She tiptoed past the marsh grass where a covey of quail nested. Continuing on, she came to the place where Grandma sat, weaving a basket. Behind Grandma was the basket stand. The stand was made of weathered wooden boards, crudely nailed together. Sheets of tin covered the rafters, making a roof. There were baskets of every size and shape hanging from hooks of long nails. Almost out of breath, Keisha asked, "Grandma, any customers today?"

Without missing a weave, Grandma answered, "Why, yes, child. I sold two baskets before noon."

"Who bought them?"

"A woman from Pittsburgh. She had seen the baskets in the city, and wanted a basket for herself and one for a friend. I sold her a fruit basket and a sewing basket. She didn't even try to haggle."

"That's great," Keisha said, as she fingered the sweetgrass piled near her grandma's chair. For as long as she could remember, she had watched Grandma weave the baskets. She secretly wanted to make one.

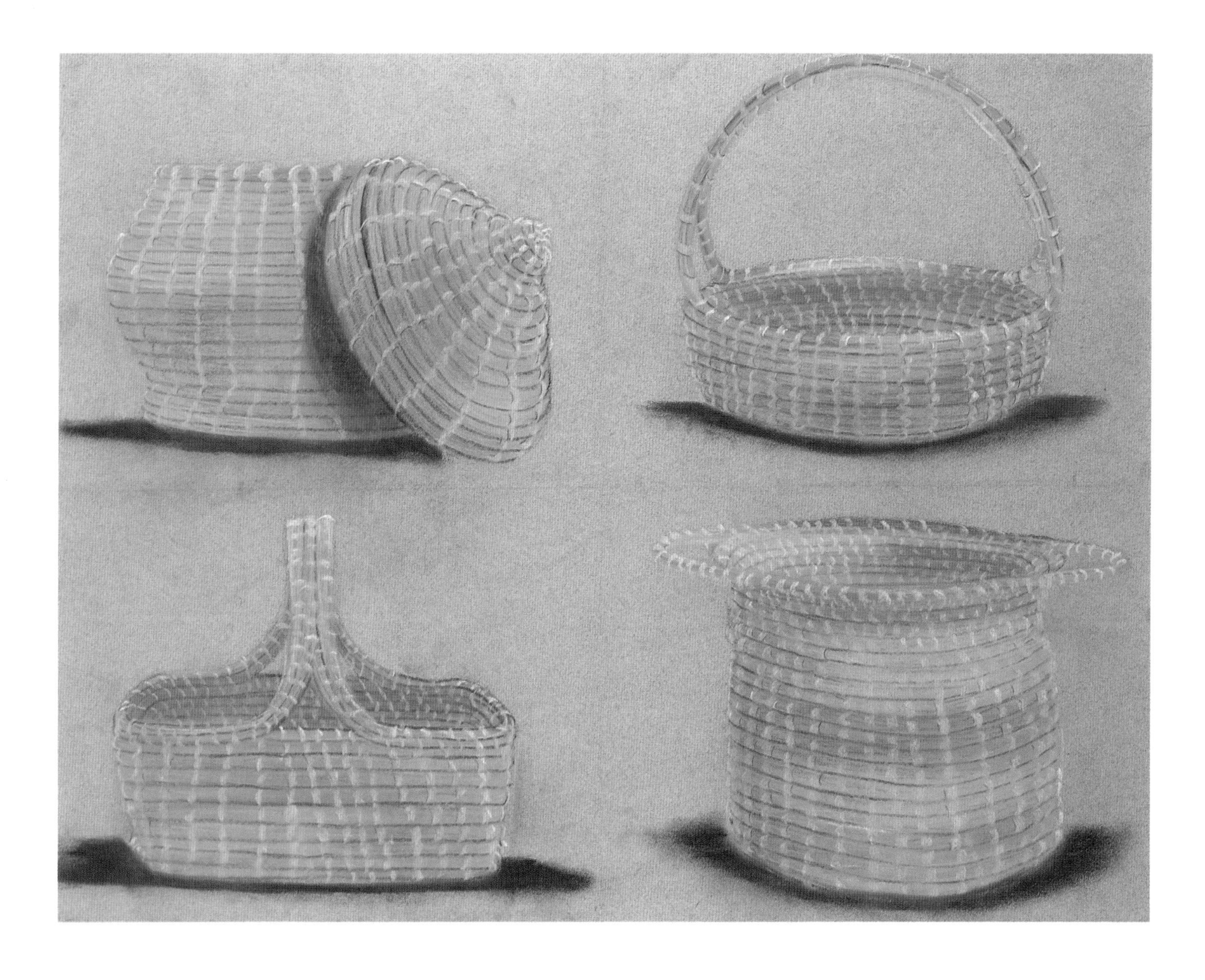

Gathering up courage, she asked, "Grandma, when can I make a basket?"

Grandma put down her half-finished basket, reached out, and pulled Keisha to her knees. Smiling at her granddaughter, she said, "Why, child, I've wanted to teach you basket weaving for a long time. I was about to think that not one of my household kin was interested in carrying on basketmaking. I made my first basket when I was just about your age. I can remember it like it was yesterday. My mama taught me just like her mama had taught her many years before."

Grandma picked up the unfinished basket and continued to weave as she talked.

"You just watch a while, and, when I finish this fruit basket, I'll help you get started. You'll first have to make the bottom, a coil, like a coaster, before you can make a full basket."

"That's fine with me," Keisha responded excitedly. "I just want to learn."

© 94

Standing beside her grandmother's chair, Keisha watched the callused hands and tireless fingers move the palmetto palm strips over the sweetgrass and pine needles. Over and in, over and in.

"You sure can weave fast, Grandma," said Keisha.

"Not as fast as I used to," Grandma replied. "I've been sewing sweetgrass baskets for might near seventy years. Your great grandma taught me all about basket weaving. She was taught by her mama who had learned it while living on the plantation. They made work baskets back then. That was when the *fanner* basket was used for cleaning the rice on the rice plantations. My mama told me sweetgrass weaving came straight from Africa long before the Revolutionary War, and it is only found in the Low Country of South Carolina."

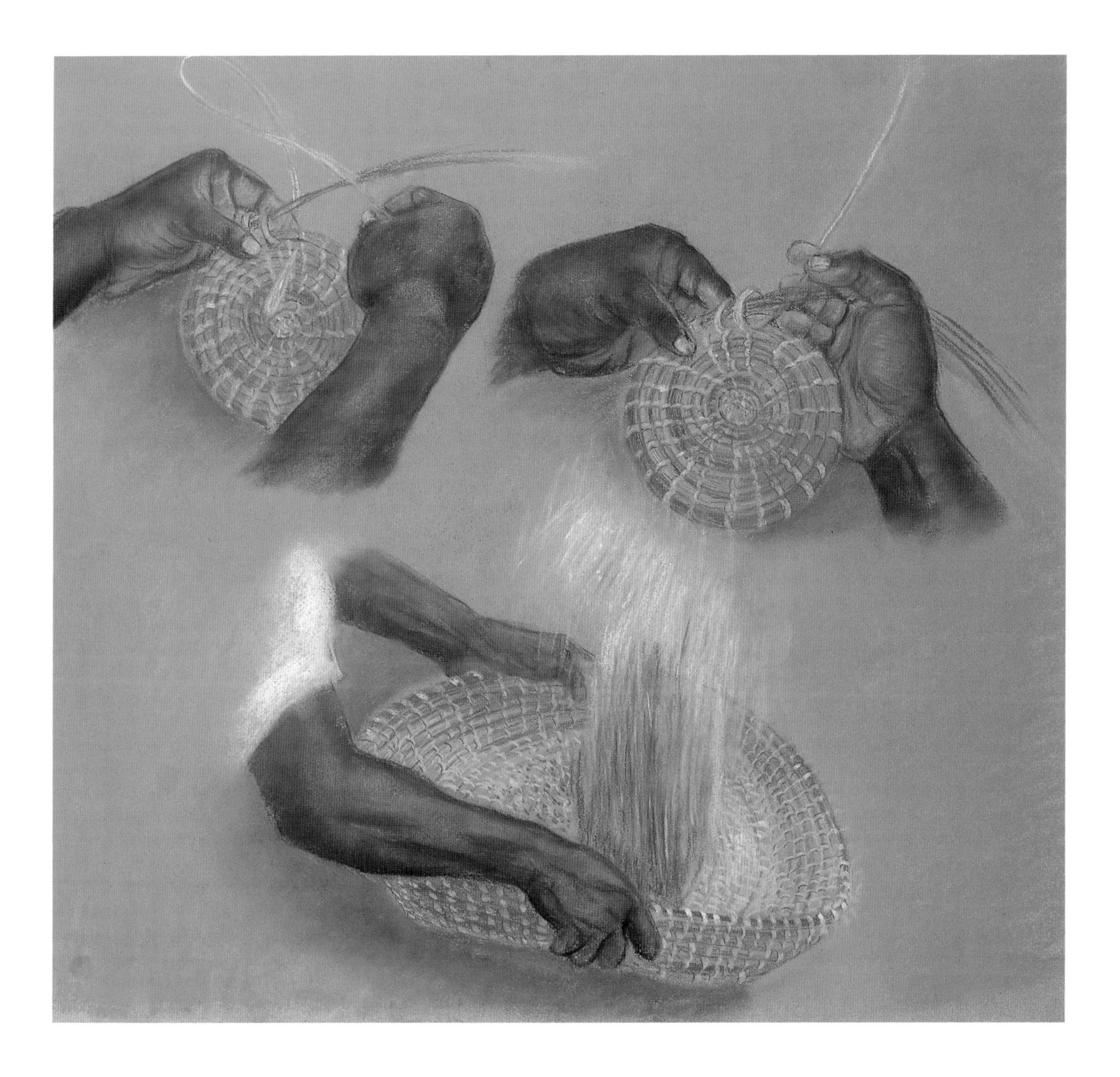

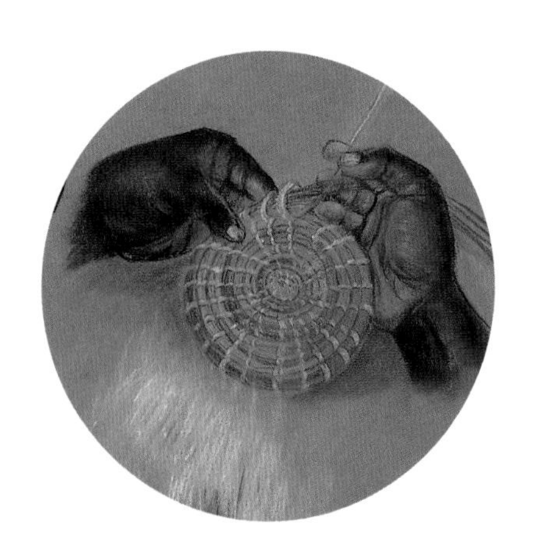

Grandma made a loop knot to tie off the end of the sweetgrass. She carefully wrapped a palm leaf strip over and in to finish the basket. Placing the finished basket on the bench beside her, she said, "Honey, I'm so happy that one of my family wants to carry on basket weaving. I was afraid it would end with my generation, since no one had ever showed interest until now.

"Take your mama. I tried to teach her when she was knee-high, but she showed no interest. All she wanted was to play with the palm leaves and pine needles. And as soon as she finished high school she went off to the city to work. Same with your Aunt Etta. She moved to New York to teach school. Too busy for baskets. You will be blessed carrying basket weaving on for your old grandma."

Keisha leaned over and hugged Grandma and said, "I'll do my best. Let's get started."

A door slammed. Keisha looked toward the house. She saw Raymond walking hurriedly in their direction.

Running to meet her brother, she began telling him all about Grandma's customer and about how Grandma was going to teach her to weave a basket.

"Slow down, sister, you're too excited," Raymond said. "Here's a biscuit for you."

"Thanks, Raymond. I thought you were helping Big Papa."

"He's already finished the garden and is resting on the back steps. I decided to come see how things are going up here."

Keisha took a bite of her biscuit. Raymond sat down on the bench near Grandma's chair. "Grandma, Keisha said you sold two baskets. How much did you get for them?"

Gently nodding her head, she said, "Enough, son. Enough."

"More than five bucks?"

"Much, much more. Why are you so interested?"

"Grandma, can men make baskets?" he asked.

"Sure they can," Grandma replied. "Your great grandpa was one of the best basket weavers this side of the river. He made work baskets, ones big enough to tote vegetables. There's one of his old baskets in the attic. I'll show it to you sometime. Folk don't weave work baskets around here anymore. Most of the basket weavers in Mount Pleasant make show baskets, using sweetgrass and palmetto palm leaf, adding longleaf pine needles for strength and color. The bulrush is used too, but not me. No sirree, not as long as your daddy and Big Papa can still find sweetgrass around the islands.

"You know, with all the buying up of the coastal lands, the sweetgrass is getting hard to find. Some basket weavers are going as far as Florida to buy it. And it's mighty expensive. It's a crying shame. Without sweetgrass this African craft would be lost forever. Things may be looking up for us basket weavers though. Last fall the Historic Charleston Foundation gave land on James Island for planting sweetgrass. If it takes on, there'll be plenty of sweetgrass for basket weavers in the future."

FOR
SALE

"That's great! I didn't realize till now that basket weaving was such a great part of my heritage. May I make a basket, too?"

"Sure you can."

Keisha wiped her mouth on her sleeve and blurted, "Oh, no you don't, Raymond! Grandma's going to teach me first."

"Now, now, Keisha. I can teach you both. You watch me carefully as I begin a basket."

Grandma reached down and picked up a small bundle of sweetgrass. First, she tied a knot in the center of the bundle. She then folded the free ends together and began to wind them around into one piece to begin the coil. Gripping the work firmly in her left hand, she pierced an opening in the center knot with the broken end of a spoon handle. She picked up a strip of palm leaf and drew it up through the opening to anchor the first coil. She repeated the steps and the coils began to spiral out from the center knot, looking much like the spokes of a wheel. As she began the fourth coil, she added more sweetgrass and handed it to Keisha.

"Hold it tightly. . . . That's my girl," she said encouragingly. She watched Keisha pierce a hole with the spoon handle and weave the palmetto palm leaf over and in, over and in.

"It's not as easy as it looks," Keisha said. "It makes my fingers hurt."

Grandma patted Keisha's hand. "It takes practice—practice and time. Your fingers have to get used to it. You mustn't overdo on your first try."

Raymond sat patiently watching his sister sew her first sweetgrass. He had not noticed the sun sinking lower and lower in the West.

"Grandma, it's my turn. I can do it now," he said.

"I'm sure you can," said Grandma, "but you're going to have to wait until after supper. Your mama and daddy will be home in a few minutes from work, and I've got to put my baskets away and cook. I'll help you start your basket right after we eat."

Taking out just enough sweetgrass, pine needles, and palmetto leaf strips to begin a coil for Raymond, Grandma picked up the basket that contained her materials. Handing it to her grandson, she said, "Take this, Raymond. I'll get the baskets from the stand. You, too, Keisha."

Keisha stopped her weaving and proudly placed the coiled bottom into Grandma's finished basket. Then she began gathering baskets from the stand.

This was a job she had done as long as she could remember. But today it was different. Today the baskets seemed more beautiful. They were no longer just Grandma's work. Today, the baskets were an art. An art that could be traced back to her ancestors, back to Africa.

With an armful of baskets, Keisha walked behind Grandma toward the house. As she walked, she heard a quail call. It seemed to say, "Weave right, weave right."

When she reached the porch, Keisha put the baskets into the storage bins. Carefully holding her coil in one hand, she opened the screen door. Grandma was already in the kitchen.

Keisha seated herself at the kitchen table and began to weave again. Grandma stirred cornmeal to make a corn pone. There was a sudden bump and a thump as Raymond rushed down the attic stairs into the kitchen. In his arms he carried a large basket.

"I found it! I found it!" he cried. "I found Great-Grandpa's basket!"

"You surely did," said Grandma, "and a fine one it is indeed!"

Keisha ran to the basket and looked inside. She saw something that Raymond had not seen. There, inside Great-Grandpa's basket, was a much smaller basket.

Picking it up, she said, "Look, Grandma, a sweet little basket. Where did it come from?"

Grandma wiped her hands on her apron and picked up the basket.

"Law, child, that's the first basket I ever made. I had forgotten it was still here. Looks good to be so old."

"Please, Grandma, may I have it?" asked Keisha.

"Yes, dear, I want you to have it," said Grandma, "and, Raymond, you can have Grandpa's. Now you will have part of the past as you carry on basket weaving for the family."

They both thanked Grandma for the baskets. Raymond ran out the back door to show his basket to Big Papa.

Holding Grandma's old basket close to her heart, Keisha smiled a big smile and said, "I'll keep it forever. It's a sweet, sweet basket."

Selected Bibliography

Baird, Keith E., and M. A. Twining. *Sea Island Roots*. Trenton: Africa World Press, 1991.

Carawan, Guy, and Candie Carawan. *Ain't You Got a Right to the Tree of Life? The People of Johns Island, South Carolina—Their Faces, Their Words, and Their Songs*. Athens: University of Georgia Press, 1989.

Chase, J. W. *Afro-American Arts and Crafts*. New York: Van Nostrand Reinhold, 1971.

Davis, Gerald L. "Afro-American Coil Basketry in Charleston County, South Carolina: Affective Characteristics of an Artistic Craft in a Social Context." In *American Folklife*, edited by Don Yoder. Austin: University of Texas Press, 1976.

Dewulf, Karol K. "Low Country Baskets." *Country Home*, October 1986, 67 and 73.

Jones-Jackson, Patricia. *When Roots Die: Endangered Traditions on the Sea Islands*. Athens: University of Georgia Press, 1987.

Proceedings of the Sweetgrass Conference, McKissick Museum, University of South Carolina, Columbia, South Carolina, March 1988.

Quick, David. "Art is Gift Alternative." *Post and Courier*, 8 December 1994.

Rosengarten, Dale. *Row Upon Row: Sea Grass Baskets of the South Carolina Lowcountry*. Columbia: McKissick Museum, University of South Carolina, 1986.

Sweetgrass Baskets of Mt. Pleasant, South Carolina. The Town of Mount Pleasant, South Carolina, 1994. Pamphlet distributed by the Mount Pleasant Sweetgrass Basketmakers Association.

Vlach, John Michael. *The Afro-American Tradition in Decorative Arts*. Athens: University of Georgia Press, 1990.

Together, **Margie Clary** and **Dennis Brown** have given to children and adults alike a look into the past and a journey into the hearts and souls of those proud artisans who have kept alive the traditions of the sea islands. *A Sweet, Sweet Basket* is a book you will read again and again.

About the author: **MARGIE WILLIS CLARY** is a teacher and a professional storyteller. She holds a masters degree in education. Having taught elementary school for thirty years, she now teaches at the college level. Her articles have appeared in regional journals and magazines, and she has published one volume of poetry. This is her first book of fiction.

A South Carolina native, Ms. Clary has called the Charleston area home for thirty years. She and her husband, Ralph, live on James Island, just outside the city. They have two children and three grandchildren.

Ms. Clary is actively associated with a number of national and local groups including the National Association of Storytellers, The International Reading Association, The Society of Children's Book Writers and Illustrators, and the state and local arts councils.

About the illustrator: **DENNIS LEE BROWN** is a self-taught portrait painter. He grew up in South Carolina and lives with his wife and two sons on James Island. He is employed by the College of Charleston. His paintings can be seen in several galleries in the city.

In *A Sweet, Sweet Basket*, Mr. Brown's pastels superbly illustrate the beauty and power of a timeless tradition and proud heritage. His warm, colorful images and the gentle facial expressions he has given to Keisha and Grandma enhance the charm and tenderness of this loving story.